Marvin K. Mooney Will you

PLEASE

GO

NOW!

Marvin K. Mooney Will you

PLEASE

GO

NOW!

By Dr. Seuss

A Bright & Early Book
COLLINS

L M N   789

The
time
has come.

The time has come.

The time is now.

Just go.
Go.
GO!
I don't care how.

You can go by foot.

You can go
by cow.

Marvin K. Mooney,
will you
please go now!

You can go
on skates.

You can go
on skis.

You can go
in a hat.

But
please go.
Please!

If you like
you can go
in an old blue shoe.

Just go, go, GO!
Please do, do, DO!

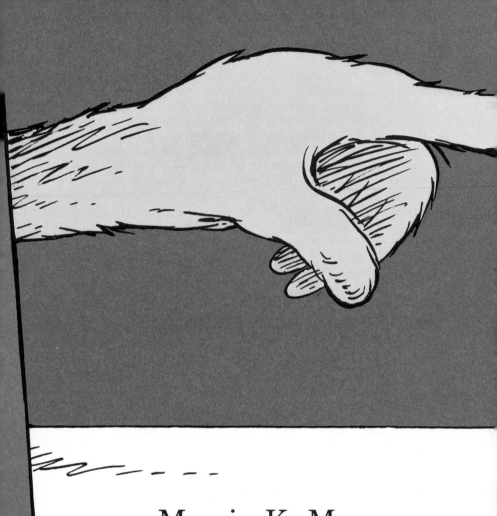

Marvin K. Mooney,
I don't care how.
Marvin K. Mooney,
will you please
GO NOW!

You can go on stilts.

You can go by fish.

You can go
in a Crunk-Car
if you wish.

If you wish
you may go
by lion's tail.

Or stamp yourself
and go by mail.

Marvin K. Mooney!
Don't you know
the time has come
to go, Go, GO!

Get on your way!
Please, Marvin K.!
You might like going
In a Zumble-Zay.

You can go
by balloon . . .

. . . or broomstick.

OR

You can go
by camel
in a
bureau drawer.

You can go by Bumble-Boat . . .

. . . or jet.

I don't care
how you go.

Just GET!

Get yourself a Ga-Zoom.

You can go with a ......

Marvin, Marvin, Marvin!
Will you leave this room!

Marvin K. Mooney!
I don't care HOW.

Marvin K. Mooney!

Will you please

GO NOW!

I said

GO

and

GO

I meant. . . .

The time had come.
SO ...
Marvin WENT.